The Stolen Child

CLARE BOYLAN

D0586985

A Phoenix Paperback

A Model Daughter first appeared in *Woman's Journal,*
and with *A Little Girl, Never Out Before* in *Concerning Virgins*
published in 1989 by Hamish Hamilton

The Stolen Child was first published in *Living*
and then in *That Bad Woman*
published in 1995 by Little, Brown

This edition published in 1996 by Phoenix
a division of Orion Books Ltd
Orion House, 5 Upper St Martin's Lane, London WC2H 9EA

ISBN 1 85799 766 2

Typeset by Deltatype Ltd, Ellesmere Port, Cheshire
Printed in Great Britain by Clays Ltd, St Ives plc

CONTENTS

A Model Daughter

'Think!' said my friend Tilly one day when we were deep into a bottle of lunchtime Meursault; 'if we had had children when we ceased to be impervious virgins they would be seventeen by now. Seventeen or thereabouts. Lovely girls!'

For a moment before her words misted into grapey vapours I could see them sitting opposite us with shiny hair and loose frocks of Laura Ashley prints.

In her early youth Tilly had been very fast and a famous mistress. She was slower now and more faithful and our friendship was occasionally shadowed by a creeping sentimentality that made me fear she would one day rush away from me and into the arms of Jesus.

'Do you regret not having had children?' I said briskly.

'I would like a girl.' She was stubborn: 'Seventeen or so.'

'You could have one. You still could.' She was forty-five but friendship entitled her to lay claim to my age, which was not quite forty.

'Have one what, darling?' Her beautiful blue eyes always had the attractive daze of myopia but after lunch and wine they shimmered under a sea haze.

'A baby!'

'A baby?' She recoiled as if someone had just thrust a seeping member of the species on to her silk knee. 'Don't be revolting!'

'Babies are where children come from,' I pointed out; a little shortly, for I had a worry of my own.

'Not necessarily,' Tilly said. 'It seems to me absurd to go to such lengths. There are young girls everywhere. In primitive countries people drown them at birth. Still they outnumber the men.' She seized the bottle and shook the dregs, very fairly, into either glass. 'If I feel the need of a daughter, I daresay I can get one somewhere.'

'But where?'

Her confidence was shaken but only for a moment. 'A model agency!'

I had a daughter. It was my one secret from Tilly. Her name was Hester and she was seventeen. My daughter was born not of love, not even of sex, but of necessity. I married Victor when I was twenty and we were both pretending to be actors, knowing perfectly well that one day we would have to grow up and get ourselves proper jobs. Six months later, to everyone's surprise, he got a break and was summoned to America. He fell in love, to no one's surprise, with his leading lady. The divorce was quick and uncontested. Shamed by my failure I kept my mouth shut and my head down. I got a small settlement and descended into that curious widowhood of the heart which an early broken marriage brings.

I was too lethargic to work and faced a frugal living on my mean allowance. 'If you had a child,' my mother scolded, 'he would have to pay a proper maintenance.' Even in this I had failed. 'Well I can't just manufacture a child!' I cried. Mother made a face as if tasting some invisible treat inside her mouth. 'Pity,' she said.

'Dear Vic,' I wrote, alone in my little room by the gas fire. He no longer seemed dear to me. I had grown sullen and immune to attachments. 'I did not want to tell you this earlier as I had no desire to destroy your happiness as you have mine, but I am expecting our child. I am letting you know now only because money is short and it will be so difficult to work.'

Vic was generous. He was a successful actor now and relieved by my faint-heartedness. A card arrived, offering congratulations, and a decent-sized cheque which was to be repeated monthly.

I didn't bother Vic much after that except in due course to announce that Hester had been born and from time to time when I badly needed a bit of extra money (for a furry coat in a really dreadful winter; for a Greek cruise because Tilly was urging me to accompany her) and then I would say that Hester had a little illness or needed her teeth straightened or that she was plaguing me for pony lessons. Once, after his second marriage had broken up, he wrote and asked if he could come and meet Hester. After a momentary panic I answered with a very firm 'no'. I had never asked him to come to her side when she was ill, I pointed out. It would be unfair of him to disturb our peaceful lives.

He accepted this, with a sort of written sigh. 'Just send me a picture of her,' he said. I was shaken, but underneath the dismay there grew a kind of excitement. I said earlier that I had grown immune to attachments. In fact it was merely romantic attachments to which I was resistant, and my friend Tilly consumed enough sexual adventure for both of us. I had a deep secret attachment to my Hester. As soon as Vic asked for her picture I realized that I too had longed to know what she looked like.

I began to carry a camera round. I sought Hester in restaurants, outside schools, in bus queues. One day I was seated in the park in the shade when a child came and looked at me; a solemn dark-eyed girl with a pink dress and a little shoulder bag of white crochet work. I snapped the child and smiled at her. She stood, quite still and graceful, fulfilling her role. I closed the shutter on my camera and closed my eyes too, to carry the moment past its limits so that she came right up to me and called me Mama. When I looked again, the girl was gone.

I wonder how often Victor looked at the picture I sent him, if he kept it in his breast pocket close to his heart; if he placed some of his hopes on that unknown child. I know I did. It helped to pass a decade swiftly and quite sweetly. Soon I was heading up to forty, the extremes of my youth gone (but not regretted) and I found myself thinking idly that Hester would be leaving school by now and we might be planning her college years. I liked this fantasy for the placing of Hester in Oxford or Cambridge would make her actual absence more plausible and allow me to enjoy my dreams with no disturbance from the dull utilities of fact.

'Dear Vic,' I wrote. 'It is some time since I have been in touch but the years have flown and we were so busy, Hester and I, with work and school, that we had no time to consider the world outside our own little one. However, the news now is too big to keep to myself. Our girl has won a First to Oxford. I want you to know that I sustain no bitterness in regard to our marriage for Hester has been a true compensation. I only wish I could indulge her with all the silly clothes students love and a little flat of her own where she could invite her grown-up friends for coffee.'

It would have been a better letter (I would have been a better person) without the embellishment of that final sentence but the truth is I got carried away and there really was a nice little flat which Tilly had been urging me to snap up.

Vic wrote back immediately. 'Wonderful news! Of course my daughter shall have everything she wants but this time I am determined to deliver it (and my congratulations!) in person.' He announced a date when he would arrive and named the restaurant where we would meet for a celebration dinner.

I suffered several moments of deep shock before my brain broke into demented activity. How should I forestall him? My first thought was a death. Hester dead in a tragic horseback accident! But he would want to see her burial place. Besides, I could not bear that loss myself. I could say she had gone abroad with friends for the summer. Vic was rich. He would insist on following her there.

Nothing I could think of was any use. All my little plans fell apart in the face of Victor's strength of purpose and superior cash flow. Besides, I did not entirely want to put him off for there was the bait of Hester's pocket money. I felt it was a point of honour to collect it safely.

On several occasions I was tempted to confide in Tilly but Tilly is like a viper on the subject of superficial friendships and I knew she would find it impossible to forgive my years of concealment. However, I stuck close to her in those worrying weeks, hoping that I might find the courage to blurt it all out or that she might inadvertently produce an anecdote or experience which would prove the solution to my dilemma. It was exactly four days before Vic's arrival that Tilly, in vino, produced her unlikely veritas of maternal regret and provided me with an answer.

A model agency! I had often glanced through fashion magazines when goaded by Tilly into visiting a hairdresser and I knew those purveyors of fantasy by sight. I was not especially interested in clothes so I gave my attention to the girls who showed them. Unlike Tilly, I did not envy them their taut busts and tiny backsides, their perfect skin and carefully arranged clouds of careless hair. It was their determination that made me wistful.

Their qualification, apart from beauty, which can be used

or abused in so many ways, was epitomized by an enduring personality which helped them adhere to a diet regime of meagre, proteinous scraps, to drink prickly Perrier instead of easeful gin, to go to bed at ten o'clock rather than allow themselves to be lured on some exciting, promiscuous prowl. It was more or less how I had pictured Hester.

All I needed was a sweet young girl to help me through a single evening. I know Victor. His passions are burning but brief. Once he had met his daughter, he could peacefully forget all about her.

'I want a girl,' I told the telephone of the Modern Beauties Agency and I gave it the date; 'just for an evening.'

'Daywear, beach or evening?' said a voice.

'Just a simple dinner dress.' I was slightly taken aback.

'Own shoes or shoes supplied?

'One was rather hoping she might have a pair of her own.'

'Size and colouring?'

I could be confident about this, at least. I described Hester as seventeen or thereabouts, tall but slim, with dark hair and a lily-pale skin.

'It's Carmen Miranda you want,' the telephone decided. 'Will you require a hairdresser and make-up artiste?'

'Carmen Miranda? Now wait a minute!'

'Thirty-five pounds an hour and VAT. To whom shall I make out the invoice?'

'Thirty-five pounds? But. . . ! Heavens!' I had anticipated that beauty might be remunerable at about four times the rate of skilled professional housework. I had put aside £50 for the evening. At this price it would cost about £200 – an impossible sum.

'Do you want to confirm that booking or make it provisional. Miss Carmen Miranda is our top professional model. She is very much in demand.'

'No! I mean, yes, I'm sure she is. The thing is, I don't think I have made myself quite clear.' I explained that I did not really require the services of their top professional model. What I wanted – *needed*, was an ingénue, an unspoilt young girl with little or no experience. And cheaper.

'The rate is standard,' said the voice, with a new, steely edge. 'Unless, of course, you want one of our new girls who have not yet completed their training.' She mentioned something that sounded like Poisoned Personality Course and added that these incomplete models could be rented hourly at a reduced rate of twelve pounds, for experience.

'Yes, yes,' I said eagerly. 'That's just right. A young girl, barely out of school. That sounds lovely.'

'All our girls are lovely.'

'I'm sure they are. Thank you so very much. You've got the description?'

'Yes, that's no problem.'

'You've been very kind. Can you tell me who to expect?'

'I'll have to see who's free.'

On the evening of our meeting I felt more excited than on my first date with Victor. Acquiring Hester's childhood photograph had been a rewarding experience. Now I was to meet her in the flesh.

I was looking forward to seeing Victor too. I had often watched him on the television and was intrigued that his face, with its strange orange American tan, had not aged at all while his eyes had, so that he looked like a spaniel with a bulldog's gaze. 'Tricky Vicky', Tilly called my ex-husband but his unreliability did not bother me now; I wanted to hear about his exploits and to be praised for my achievement – Hester – and I was looking forward to getting some of his money. The evening had acquired an additional significance. We would meet as a successful family, untouched by the tension, the sacrifice, the quelling of self that normally accompanies family life. We had got off scot free and yet would not be exposed in loneliness.

I checked with the agency to make sure that my surrogate daughter was still available and they, wearily, assured me that Angela or Hazel or Patricia would meet me in the lounge at the appointed hour. Such nice names! Nothing could go wrong. All my little Angela or Hazel had to remember was to answer to Hester. There were no shared memories to rehearse. Vic had no experience of academic life so she would not be quizzed on that. In any case I had taken the precaution of booking the girl half an hour in advance of Vic's arrival time so that I could give her a little briefing.

It was almost that time when I was startled by the arrival in the lounge of a sort of human sunburst. Women started to wriggle and whisper. 'Good Lord,' I said ungraciously. It was Vic, thirty-five minutes early.

He cast his gaze over the women in the lounge, not really looking for me but allowing each female present to melt and open to his boyish charm. Perhaps he would not recognize me. I could slip out and wait at the exit for Hester to prime her on her role. I rose, face half averted – and drew attention to myself.

'Barbara!' His voice had gained boom and timbre. He put a little kiss on the air and flopped down casually beside me, fastidiously raising the knees of his trousers.

'Hello Vic.'

'Sorry I'm so early. First night nerves,' he said, his nose wincing appealingly under big drooping eyes. He had developed an American accent.

'That's all right. Have a drink.'

'You look good,' he said. 'How's life been treating you? What a time I had, getting here! You would think, since we were shooting in Europe . . .' And he launched, as I had imagined he would, into a story about himself.

When Hester comes, I shall rush to the door to greet her, I thought. I gave Victor my smiling mouth and my nodding head but my attention was elsewhere. I shall see a tall, pale, beautiful girl – probably shy – in the entrance and I shall run to her and put my arms around her and if she doesn't cry out for help I shall just have time to explain before we get back to the table.

10   Something Victor said brought my mind right back.

'. . . Anyway, I'm glad I got here early so we could talk about money before Hester gets here.'

'Money?'

'A sort of financial plan. I thought, twenty thousand dollars now, or five thousand a year until she's twenty-one. If you take the lump sum now you could invest it but there's less risk with an annuity.'

'Twenty thousand dollars?' My head spun as I tried out a string of noughts against the little digit and attempted to perform a dollar conversion.

'Well, I guess that's not a lot these days. What the heck – make it pounds.'

'Oh, Vic. I'm very – she'll be very grateful.'

'Say, what's she like?' Vic leaned forward and touched my knee.

'Quiet. More like me than you, I'm afraid. I hope you won't be disappointed.'

'I've been disappointed since.' The bulldog eyes attempted bashfulness. 'I wasn't disappointed then.'

We were getting along quite nicely when a wretched autograph hunter recognized Vic and hovered at his chair. She just hovered but her presence sapped one.

'Look, dear, if you don't mind . . . !' I said.

The girl glared at me. I flinched in the dull light of those purple-ringed eyes set in a yellowish face and crowned with gluey horns of hair. She wore a cheap Indian cotton anorak and an extraordinary satin dress from which her uncooked-looking breasts popped unpleasantly. Quite suddenly, tears bubbled up in her eyes. 'Aw shit,' she said and she tottered off. She did not leave the room. Her perambulation took her in the opposite direction where she paused, glancing back. Vic and I laughed uneasily and he called a waiter for champagne. He was appraising the label when the girl returned and crouched beside me, breathing wetly and heavily in my ear: 'Look, are you Mrs Marshall?'

'I am.'

'Well I'm Araminta.'

Victor was staring.

'Look here, dear . . .'

'From the agency.'

'What?'

'My real name's Angela. Araminta's my professional name – going to be.'

'No!'

'What's the matter?' Victor said.

'I think she's sick or something,' said Araminta.

'Sick!' I echoed faintly. It was not a lie. I rose and bundled my arms around the repellent Araminta. 'Please excuse us.'

Araminta and I faced each other in the uneasy pinkness of the ladies' washroom. 'You must leave immediately,' I said. 'There has been a dreadful mistake.'

'Who says? Whose mistake?' Her voice was a whine.

'You were brought here tonight to represent my daughter Hester, to celebrate with her famous father – whom she has never met before – her scholarship entrance to Oxford University.'

'That's beautiful. Like an episode from "Dallas".'

'If you think, for one instant, that you are fit to stand in the shoes of my daughter then you are even more deranged than you look. Now go away!'

'Here!' Her wail was like a suffering violin string. 'I want my money.'

'Not a penny!'

Araminta's mouth opened into a grille shape and a loud gurgle of grief issued therefrom. 'It's not my fault. No one told me I was to be your frigging daughter. I borrowed money to have me hair done an' all. What am I going to do?'

I was pondering the same question when the door opened, and Vic came in, looking confused. 'Is everything all right? Who's this?' he said of the screaming, streaming Araminta.

My soothing utterances were lost in the noise that Araminta made, of a train reversing, to sniff back her sobs. Her face was striped with purple but erased of tears. 'Hello Dad,' she said. 'I'm Hester.'

We were all congealed like the victims of Pompeii. After an eternity of seconds Vic showed signs of recovery. 'Hester?' he whispered. 'Barbara . . . ?'

I closed my eyes. I could not look at him. 'She is going through . . . a phase.'

I heard a tap running, a tiny strange bark of dismay as, presumably, some woman attempted to enter and found her path blocked by a famous heartthrob. When I could bear to look I saw Hester calmly splashing her face, 13 applying fresh scribbles of purple to her eyes and daubing her lips with mauve gloss that resembled scar tissue. Poor Vic looked badly shaken. On an impulse I seized the girl and ducked her beneath the tap again, washing every trace of colour from her skin. I scrubbed her dry on a roller towel and then patted her complexion with my own powder puff and a smear of my blusher. Her eyes, even without their purple tracing, resembled Mary Pickford's in their worse excesses of unreasoned terror. 'You some kind of frigging maniac?' she hissed. 'Shut up!' I wielded a hairbrush which I used to remove the glue from her head, and some of her hair. When I had finished there stood a tall, pale girl with wild dark hair, a little overweight, quite pretty, although her eyes and her breasts still popped nastily.

Whatever Vic was feeling he used his actor's training to conceal it. 'Come along, girls,' he said. 'It doesn't do for an actor to get himself arrested in the ladies' loo!'

Hester cawed with mirth.

Back in the restaurant there was a period of peace while Hester ate and Victor brooded. The girl appeared to be ravenously hungry. She did not pay any attention to us until a first course and several glasses of wine had scuttled down her throat and her cheeks were nicely padded with roast beef and then, with a coy, sideways look at Vic, she produced a classic line:

'Where have you been all my life?'

Vic eyed her gloomily. 'Hasn't your mother explained?'

'Not bloody much.'

Odd that I had not noticed before that they both had the same pessimistically protruding eye.

'I think your mother has rather a lot of explaining to do,' Vic said.

'Pardon?' I was so startled I could only squeak.

'Barbara, I am disappointed.' He put up a hand to swat a second squeak of protest which was escaping. 'Yes! I have been let down. Over seventeen years I have given unstintingly to the support of my daughter, trusting that you would bring her up as I would wish. You denied me access to her. I did not attempt to use the force of law in my favour. You did not want your lives disturbed, you said. What life? I ask you, what life have you given this girl? It is clear from her speech that she has been allowed to run wild in the streets. She's even hungry. Look how she eats! Have you anything to say?'

Very little, really. It was true the girl was appalling. 'Just be glad you haven't had to put up with her,' I snapped.

'She won't give me my money,' Hester complained. She shoved another roast potato into her mouth and seized Victor's sleeve. 'You'll give me my money, won't you?'

Victor retrieved his garment. 'Young lady, I'll give you something more valuable than money. I will give you advice. Reach for the moon – not its reflection in some puddle in the gutter. Look beyond the superficial values of youth and fashion. Stand up proud – alone if needs be. You'll have self-respect. You'll have *my* respect. What do you say, dear?'

'Vic,' I interjected, lost in our improvised drama; 'it is you who must look beyond the superficial. She has won a First to Oxford.'

'I'm not talking to you, Barbara. I'm speaking to my daughter. You know I don't believe the academic world equips you for real life. Now Hester, what do you say?'

'Why don't you ride off into the sunset on your high horse, you big ballocks?' Hester said, and she importuned a waiter for profiteroles.

Victor looked so stunned, so *dis*armed, I was almost sorry for him. 'She is overwrought,' I said. 'Think what she has achieved! She has been locked up with her books all year and now she is in . . . revolt.'

Underneath I had begun to warm to Hester. Victor was not used to challenge. My once-husband seemed quite broken by her reproach. 'You know I don't expect much,' he sighed. 'It's the simple things I like in women – feminine grace, charm and wit.'

'I'm with you, mate!' Hester spoke up through a mouthful of gunge. 'This university lark was all her idea. Personally I've always thought women would be better off burning their brains than their bras. Could I have a liqueur?'

'You mean you don't want to go to university?' I was quite hurt.

'Too bloody right. I'm really a model, you know,' she confided to Vic. 'Although what I'd like best in all the world . . .' (her eyes glittered greedily) '. . . is to be an actress.'

'You'd like to be an actress?' Vic threw me a tiny look of triumph. His expression began to brighten.

'Dearest Dad . . . !' She leaned across the table so that her breasts rested on her pudding plate like a second, uncoated helping of dessert and it began to dawn on me that she might be a little bit drunk: 'All my life I have worshipped you from afar. My one dream has been to emul . . . follow in your hallowed footsteps.'

Vic smiled. His bulldog's gaze flickered with warmth and interest. Their eyes, inches apart, wobbled glassily. The child's look grew positively rakish and I had to kick her under the table to remind her of her filial role.

'Chip off the old block!' Vic said in admiration and he patted her pudgy hand.

'Thank you, Daddy.' Hester wrinkled her nose in exactly the way he often does.

'Would you really like to go on the stage?' he said.

'More than anything – except of course, the movies.'

'Then the movies it's going to be. I'm bringing you back with me.'

'No!' I moaned.

'You mean it?' Hester said.

'I can get you a small part in the film I'm working on. Just a walk-on but it will be a start. Come back to America with me and we'll get you into stage school. I'll make Hollywood sit up and take notice of my beautiful daughter.'

Hester glowed so that, in the flattering candlelight, she 17 did look rather beautiful. I felt depressed. Vic was taking my daughter away. There would be no more secret dreams for me; and no more money.

'Of course we'll have to tidy you up a bit!' Victor had advanced to practical planning. 'You're going to have to learn to speak properly and I'm afraid, darling, you'll have to lose some of those curves. First thing tomorrow you're going on a diet. I want you skinny as a stalk of celery before we go back.'

At this Hester's face began to alter shape, the jaw extending, the eyes receding into pink slits, the mouth widening and lengthening. We watched in awe until a horrible howl came out. 'I can't!' she wailed. 'I'm pregnant!'

It was some time before I saw my friend Tilly again. There was such a lot to do with the baby coming and poor Vic in such a state. 'I insist that you tell me everything. Everything!' he had said in the restaurant after Hester dropped her bombshell, and of course the wretched girl did.

She has gone now. I think it's for the best. She ate such a lot and would answer only to Araminta. In any case now that the baby is born it would be confusing to have two Hesters in the house.

In the end Araminta did go back to America with Vic. No longer father and daughter, they had found a new role which seemed to suit both of them much better. And Vic left me really a very generous allowance for the child.

I hope I have explained my story clearly to you for I simply cannot seem to make Tilly understand. 'Good God, darling,' she said, peering with fascinated horror into the pram on the day I introduced her to the infant. 'Did I never tell you about the Pill?'

And there was Hester, so sweet and solemn in her frills, her hands waving like pink sugar stars; her life stretched out before us, its mysterious curves and dazzling prospects, its sunlit patches and shadows, like the carriage drive to some enchanting manor.

I tried once more to tell my friend about my daughter's coming, but Tilly, fearing tales of childbed, waved a dainty hand burdened with costly mineral rocks, and said: 'What matter the source of life so long as it is lived happily ever after.'

She is right of course, for which of us anyway ever truly understands where babies come from.

A Little Girl, Never Out Before

Mrs Deveney had a yellow face and lips like withered lupins. When she smiled her lips went down at the corners but the yellow ridges of her teeth stayed behind. Her eyes were like two tarnished salt spoons. She asked Frankie had she any religion and Frankie, echoing her mother, said that religion was for orphans and spinsters. She wanted to know what Frankie knew and Frankie said she couldn't say until she was asked. After that Mrs Deveney went mad entirely. 'You are an ignorant rip,' she told the little girl, 'who may take herself back home to her heathen of a mother.'

'Yes ma'am,' Frankie said, relieved, but when Mrs Deveney had finished going mad and had spun little ropes of white spit between her teeth she told Frankie to get up the stairs to Lena who would show her where she was to sleep and tell her her duties.

After her husband's death Mrs Deveney had opened a rooming house. It gave her an interest in life, which was an interest in making money. She advertised board and residence, superior; piano: £1 weekly. She mentioned its suitability for honeymooners, its view of the cattle mart, a speciality of home-made brown bread. She made the bread herself. It was not so much brown as a sort of greenish yellow with a sourness which was her particular gift.

The actual work of the house was done by a cook and kitchen maid. She gave these girls time off for their religious duties and warm washing water every Saturday, but her goodness was wasted. A week before she had to get rid of Brid Feeney (with her big backside, like a married woman's) when she found her sitting on the edge of Mr McMahon's bed – a teacher – giving his back a scratch. It was not the suggestiveness of the situation that outraged her so much as the nerve of a serving girl making herself familiar with an educated man. It was the lack of proper deference to the male sex.

Brid Feeney only laughed at her; she said it wasn't the dark ages, it was the turn of the century. Mrs Deveney disliked the phrase. It made her think of milk on the turn. The world was turning bad. The past decades had brought flying machines, motor cars, electric lighting, defying the laws of nature and flying in the face of God. She still believed in the old ways, in sentimental values.

She found the little girl through a notice in *Freeman's Journal*. Up to this she had taken girls sent to her by the nuns but the sisters had a redemptive mission and she had a suspicion that they caught their girls in the act of falling. There was something worldly and sniggering about them. They lacked the humility that was proper to the poor.

When she applied herself to the newspaper columns, 21

therefore, she was looking for something more than a kitchen maid. She was seeking a phrase, a niceness.

'A rabbit trapper – has been brought up to it. Highest references from gentleman.' 'Mrs Harford will teach new beginners the pianoforte.' 'Good cook, thoroughly understands her business.' Lena's hard toast crackled beneath Mrs Deveney's porcelain teeth and she softened it wistfully with a mouthful of tea. Downstairs she could hear that same horse of a one bawling that Jesus Mary and Joseph she only had one pair of hands as some couple from the country complained of having to go hungry on their honeymoon.

'An orphan (16) from school, wishes to go to a lady where she would be taught to be a servant;' and then – 'A respectable little girl, never out before.'

She explored the notion of herself as a lady but then she thought, sixteen was very old for an orphan to be looking for work. Already she had probably left a brace of triplets in some other orphanage.

She liked the idea of a little girl, never out before. She pictured something as new and unprinted as the Holy Communion wafer, unspoilt, unknowing, modest, and cheap.

The little girl turned out small for her age. She said she was twelve but looked not more than ten. Her brown pinafore had a lifeless look, which was common to the clothing of the poor and came not, as people imagined, from infrequent washing but from insufficient rinsing as water had to be carried up from a yard and the whole wash was rinsed in a single tub. She folded her hands in front of her but they kept unfolding and grasping at air as if she was used to holding a doll.

Lena showed her the wooden box where she was to keep her underwear and her shoes and a nail on the wall for her coat. There was a wardrobe but it was full of Lena's things – clothes and boxes and romantic novelettes. A basin of cold water was left on top of the wooden box for weekday washing but Lena said she never washed until Saturdays, except her hands which Mrs D inspected twenty times a day.

Lena complained that Mrs D expected them to strip down to their raw bones every night and then undress in the morning again for washing but she herself kept her underwear on day and night as the cold was brutal. She advised Frankie to do the same as she didn't want to have to look at her raw bones. Since Lena looked like a fat white fish with pendulums of flesh adorning her jaws and tiny rows of greasy brown ringlets, Frankie was quite agreeable to this arrangement.

The cook was an immense country girl of twenty-two or three. She moved slowly and had small brown eyes. When she recited the litany of rough work that was to fill Frankie's days, the little girl couldn't help thinking it left hardly anything at all for Lena herself to do. All the same the cook had a secret which Frankie recognized right away. In the disappointing house she would wear it against her chest like a locket.

'Get up at 6.30 winter, six o'clock in summer, open shutters, light range, lay breakfast tables, sweep and dust drawing room and supply all rooms with coal,' Lena recited. 'Clean all the flues, black lead kitchen range, wash out kitchen boiler, clean thoroughly the hall, kitchen stairs, passage and water closets. Take cans of hot water to every room. Empty slops.' Lena showed Frankie the house as she reeled off the kitchen maid's responsibilities. Frankie appraised gaunt curtains in the cheerless colours of dried blood or dried peas, the mismatched furniture and pictures of stags or saints bleeding on the walls.

'Never go into the boarders' rooms without knocking,' Lena warned her. 'There's married couples in some.'

'I know all about that,' Frankie was glad to know something, although it would be hard not to know when you lived in one room with your ma and da and the young ones.

'Maybe you know too much.' Lena folded her arms. 'Maybe you think you're Miss Hokey Fly eighteen ninety-nine. Well let me put this in your pipe. It's me be's in charge round here and if anything is took or stole, it's you'll be blempt.'

The older girl went out into the back yard and leaned against a lavatory shed with a festering smell. She hummed a tune that was popular in Dan Lowry's. 'Have you your women's monthlies yet?' Frankie nodded. 'Mine have went,' Lena remarked, 'but they were a nuisance.' She was disappointed that the new girl was only a child. She seemed too young even for teasing. 'What are you thinking, Hokey Fly?'

'The house,' Frankie said. 'It isn't much, is it?'

'What were you expecting, uniformed butlers and electrical lights?'

She had been expecting a garden with asters and dahlias, an apple tree.

The child gave her the pickle, Lena decided, with her delicate lady's air and her rotten span of attention. 'Have you got any questions, Hokey, or do you know it all by now?'

She plucked back her attention from an upstairs window where a long-faced woman stood fastening the throat of an opossum cape. 'Do we get much to eat?' she said.

The little girl sat on the edge of the bed in the dark, her blanket wrapped around her shoulder, her bare legs dangling over the edge. Unknown to sun or sky, it was morning. She had slept a little towards dawn, a dizzy sickly doze, and then woken in a panic because the baby was missing. She always slept with it in her arms and they woke up wet but warm. In the day she carried the infant while she cleaned up or cooked and her hands were formed to its support.

When she opened her eyes she thought she was at home because of the loud, gurgling snores that were like her da's but it was Lena. Lena was who she lived with now. She wondered when she'd ever see her ma again, or cuddle the baby. Ah, she missed her ma. She cried for a few minutes, wiping her eyes and nose with her blanket, but Lena reached out her big knobby foot and gave her a kick so she pulled on her brown pinafore and her stockings and boots and went down to light the range.

Her room was in the attic of the house and she crept down its five storeys in the dark, past the snuffling creaking married couples, past the yearning schoolteacher and the long-faced woman with the opossum cape, past the dark dining room and drawing room which waited in silence to claim life from her fidgeting hands.

The cold possessed her like a drowning. She felt her way to the kitchen and stood there in the dark. Lena had not shown her where to find matches. Who can tell what hides in the dark of old kitchens, scuttling about with mice and mould and skins of dripping? The sounds that live inside total silence are the worst in the world. She crept around, her fingers touching things that felt horrible – soaking porridge, tea leaves in a sieve. Her breath came out in persevering grunts. At last she grasped a match and lit the kitchen lamp. It leaked a little pool of yellow light and monsters swarmed up the wall. She knelt on the floor and began to rake out the ashes.

It was her mother's idea that she should go to work in a big house. They were pals. They comforted each other with sweet tea and the flesh of babies. Her da was always after her ma, all the time. They could have stopped him, disabled him with a knife or a chair, but they had a weakness. They both loved infants, newborn. No matter that there wasn't even enough for the existing ones to eat, Frankie and her ma saw infants as the marvel of the world. It was worth all the hurting and the hunger to have another, brand new, every other year.

They were a hopeless pair, she and her ma. When her father had gone out for the day and the middle ones were in school Frankie would climb back into bed beside her. They kept themselves warm with the two little ones. They dreamed of the feasts they might eat if there was ever any money, but they didn't bother all that much. Hunger was just a fact of their life, and there were rewards.

It was after Frankie got her women's monthlies that the notion arose of sending her away. She was growing into a lady now, her ma said. It was time to learn a lady's life.

Her ma said that she would learn the quality of fine silver and how to stitch linen. She would eat blancmange and cold beef in the kitchen. She would gather roses in a wicker basket and arrange them on a polished table by a long window. It became their new dream, after the dreams of food. In idle fancy they walked under wedding-cake ceilings, exploring the rooms, peeking into bureaux to spy on love letters, opening the lids of golden boxes to admire jewels or bon bons or cigars inside. They mooned over the young man of the house who was kind but distant, concealing emotion beneath a brittle moustache as he played at the piano.

She didn't look any more like a lady than she had the year

before. Her legs were sticks and her chest was flat as a wash board. All the same she was growing up and her father knew it too. Sometimes when he came in from his night's drinking and had performed gravely in the bucket in the corner, he would reach not for Ma but for Frankie, his dimmed senses directed by nostalgia to the spring scent of womanhood and not its spent season.

She stuffed the stove's ugly gob with coke and papers and stood over it while it lit, shivering and warming her legs as she tempted it with morsels of twisted paper and a sprinkling of sugar the way her mother had shown her. By the time it was lighting the kitchen clock said a quarter past seven and she had to run to catch up. There was no time to wash her hands when she finished the fires so that the breakfast plates and saucers were branded by her black prints as she set the tables.

In all their uncertain fantasies of grandeur the one thing Frankie and her ma had been sure of was that there would be enough to eat in a big house. Poor Ma wouldn't believe it if she told her she had nothing since her tea yesterday, which was two slices of the sour brown bread smeared with marge. There would be no more until after the boarders had eaten breakfast, when she could have some of the porridge that remained.

The poor learn to live with hunger by moving slowly and sleeping a lot but she had hardly slept and she had to run all the time to keep up with the work. As she set out the bread and sausages and rings of black pudding for Lena to cook for breakfast, her fingers fell to temptation and stealthily fed her a slice of bread. After that she went upstairs to knock up the married couples.

Mrs Deveney was pleased with the little girl's first day. She wasn't sociable. She did not look at the male boarders nor loiter on the landings with Lena. In spite of her dreamy air, she was thorough. Her fires did not go out. An inspection of the dishes she washed revealed no scabs of oatmeal, no rusty stains of tea. She summoned Frankie after she had finished making the beds and emptying the slops. The child looked dazed. Her face was a panic stricken white and her hands black as the devil. 'What are you?' Mrs Deveney asked her briskly.

'I'm a girl.' Frankie looked surprised. 'A maid.' She knew nothing. She had answered wrong. She waited patiently while the lupin lips wove themselves into a shape for contumely.

'You are a filthy, thieving little tinker of the common lower orders,' Mrs Deveney said.

Frankie looked at the big black piano, as fat and listless as a funeral horse. She wondered if the boarders ever dared to use it, if one of the silent men at breakfast might serenade his new wife, while she leaned across the lid to show him her breasts.

Oft in the stilly night . . . Her mother used to sing that long ago. She wondered what her ma was doing now. Was the baby fretting for her?

'Look at me!' snapped Mrs Deveney. 'Explain yourself.' 29

A bag of bones her da used to say, until she began to turn into a lady. A flock of dreams. A waking ghost. A gnaw of hunger.

'You left filthy black fingerprints all over the breakfast china and you stole a slice of bread.'

'I was hungry,' Frankie said, and then, invaded by curiosity; 'how did you know?'

'The nerve of you! Every stim in this house is counted. The bread is cut the night before – two slices for every boarder. It was Lena who informed me of the robbery.'

Mrs Deveney demanded to know why Frankie had not worn gloves while doing the dirty work of the house, the grates and the slops, and declared that she had brought a breath of depravity into a good Catholic household. She believed it too but did not add that it was a matter of routine. All the servants stole. She expected it and kept their rations meagre knowing that thieving was in their nature and that they would steal food whether they needed it or not.

In a matter of weeks Frankie would grow cunning and learn to conceal evidence of her enterprise. Lena was by now an accomplished bandit. Search as she might Mrs Deveney could only find clues to modest pilferage yet the girl grew fatter by the hour.

Was ever a slice of bread so richly mourned? The little salt-spoon eyes seemed to corrode yet further as rebuke buzzed from the withered lips. And still she was hungry. She
thought about the newest baby, Doris, whose eyes were not

like salt spoons but like measured sips of a morning sky. At first those eyes had been blind and it was her little ruched mouth that pondered but in a little while everything was lit up by their wonder as if they saw the face of God, if you believed in that sort of thing, or a fairy.

Jack was next, named by their father after the boxer Jack Kilraine, the Terror of the Age, but their Jack was only two and had not yet fulfilled his father's hopes, having a preference for sweetened milk and women's bodies. There was Ethel and Mick, aged six and ten. Frankie loved them all and felt gratified by their need of her. She was proud to be her mother's protector. She had no desire for an independent life. Her own needed her. They always would. She thought of them all alone, with no one to comfort them or cook for them, and panic gripped at her knees. Who would cheer her ma up in the morning after her da had gone, leaving the trail of his temper, a smell of beer and the dank aftermath of his night-time business?

She always lay on the bed looking cold and sort of grey until Frankie brought her tea and opened the windows and sang a few songs and lit up the ashes in the grate.

Christmas was only six weeks off and the small ones were already counting. Frankie was the one who made the ginger biscuits and scrounged for oranges to put in the children's stockings. It was she who saved up new pennies, one for each child.

'I'm going home now,' she said in her offhand way. 'My ma will be wanting me.'

'Ah, now,' the widow looked alarmed. 'Your mammy is depending on the few shillings. You'd only be letting her down.'

'No I wouldn't,' Frankie said. 'My ma loves me.'

'Of course she does,' Mrs Deveney forced her mouth down into a smile. 'You're only in want of refinement and religion. You should pin your hair up and maybe I'd make you a present of a gown for Sundays. Brid Feeney's grey could be cut down for you. I'm going to give you time off to go to Mass and confession with Lena. What do you say?'

Frankie shook her head. She was too tired. She only wanted to go home.

'And if you were loyal to me, of course, you would get a nice present at Christmas – something you could bring home to benefit your poor little brothers and sisters. Say "yes ma'am".' Her smile vanished when she saw ambition enter Frankie's dreamy eye. 'Say "thank you, ma'am".'

She got used to the wearing of household gloves, the smell of chloride of lime and the racking bouts of grief that she carried carefully to the outside lavatory. She learned to steal things that could not be counted, spoons of starch or custard powder, a fistful of dry oatmeal.

The married couples came and went, their honeymoons accomplished with relief, if not much comfort. McMahon the schoolteacher stayed on. Sometimes he invited Frankie into his room, but she said she wasn't allowed. The boys who came to the back door with fish or groceries tried to grapple with her but she was a good kicker. Anyway, they preferred Lena who developed a kind of glamour in the hands of men, allowing them to feel her giant bosoms or anything they liked.

Once she surprised her in the pantry with a bakery lad. The youth and the massive girl turned to gawp at her. 'Get out! Get away you dirty little scut, you cur,' Lena snarled.

'You'll get a baby if you do that,' Frankie told her.

'Don't you be ridiculous,' Lena said. 'How could I get a baby now.'

Frankie laughed, which earned her a blow on the ear. There was no argument to that.

Within a month she had begun to turn into one of those wiry little workers, who are silent and swift and indispensable. Mrs Deveney kept her word and came up the five flights of stairs, carrying, with caution and difficulty, her Christmas gift.

It was a little house or shed. The roof was thatched like those of the poor cottagers who lived in the hills, and animals wandered around inside. A poor little baby slept in a pigsty or something.

'What is it?' Frankie said. She had been hoping for money or a box of biscuits, something for the children.

'It is the holy crib,' Mrs Deveney stood back to let the child peer inside the house where she saw that there were toy people as well as animals and the baby. Foreigners. 'What's it for?' she said.

'It is to put you in mind of the spirit of Christmas,' the widow mystifyingly declared. 'The figure in the manger is 33 baby Jesus and the lady in blue is His mother, the Virgin Mary.'

'She can't be His mother,' Frankie said; 'not if she's a virgin.'

'These are the three wise kings, led to Bethlehem by a star shining from the East, who came to worship and brought gold, frankincense and myrrh.'

'Who were they?' Frankie wondered.

'They were gifts!' Mrs Deveney tried to hide her impatience of the little girl's stupidity, for it was all as plain to her as right and wrong, but her teeth clenched and she sprayed spit. 'Gifts of inestimable value. Lena will explain.'

But all Lena explained was that Jesus Mary and Joseph they had enough junk in the room already. She picked up the little house just as Frankie was examining a mouse-sized ox. She climbed on to her own bed and heaved the crib up on top of the wardrobe.

One Sunday at Mass the little girl grew bored and slipped out of church and used the halfpenny she had been given for the collection plate to go home on a tram. She didn't have to worry about Lena, who never went to Mass anyway but loitered under a big-brimmed hat talking to corner boys.

It was a shock when she saw their room again, so cluttered, so cold. Had it always been so mingy? She stood in the doorway, looking at these poor people, trying to make them her own.

Her ma was the first to notice her. She sat up in bed, tears filling her eyes, unable to speak but silently mouthing,

'Frankie, Frankie.' She seemed astonished to see her as if she had imagined her dead or gone for ever.

'Hello, Ma,' Frankie said. 'I've come home. I'll stay if you want.'

'Ah, Frankie!' her mother found her voice. 'Aren't you a picture?'

Frankie's bones hurt from wanting to be squeezed. She wanted to run to her ma, but she couldn't, there was a restraint. She decided to make herself useful and bent before the cold fire, shovelling out the ash, putting aside any useful lumps of coke.

'Ah God!' her mother cried, 'your lovely dress! Get up, Ethie,' she nagged the younger child. 'Your sister's used to better now.'

Ethel sidled past Frankie in her greyish petticoat. She was carrying Doris. 'She's wet,' she said, and would not let her go when Frankie tried to take the baby.

'I amn't changed,' Frankie said. 'I never stopped thinking about you – every minute of every day.'

Her ma was out of bed now, pulling on her clothes. She kept having to sniff back tears. She snorted with her head stuck in the neck of her jumper.

'Da?' Frankie appealed.

Her father nodded at her politely and pulled up his blanket to cover his vest.

She wanted to hold them all, even her da. They were trying to do things for her. They cleared clothes off a chair so that she could sit down. Ethel put a cup of tea in her hand

and her mother spread a tea towel over her knee. 'To save your lovely dress,' she said.

'It's not mine,' she said. 'I only wear this of a Sunday. Mrs Deveney cut it down from the last girl. Underneath, I'm still the same.'

Her mother shook her head. 'You look the part, so you do.'

Ethel fingered the grey grosgrain bow which Mrs Deveney took from a box each Sunday morning to pin to the back of Frankie's hair. 'Can you get me one of those?' she said.

'You can have this one,' Frankie said, knowing she would be killed when she went back, if she went back.

To the family, her carelessness with ribbons was more evidence of her social success. 'Tell us dotey,' her mother said; 'what's it like, the big house?'

She would tell Mrs Deveney that a boy stole her bow outside the church – a Protestant boy.

What would she say to her mother? 'There's a garden,' she improvised. 'Roses and apples – a strawberry bed.'

'What do you eat?' her ma said. 'Do you eat strawberries?'

'Chicken,' she decided.

'You'd never fit in with us now,' her mother nodded, confirming for herself the worst. 'Not any more.'

'I would so,' Frankie said.

'You'd never fit anyhow,' her father grinned. 'Your mother hasn't told you yet. We've another one on the way.'

Frankie's ma held on to Ethel for comfort.

In the afternoon, back in the big house, the ache in her bones became a squealing. None of them had hugged her. They clutched at her Sunday gloves as she said goodbye. She helped Lena with the dinner and cleared the tables and then the Sunday afternoon silence descended and she was alone. She went up to the second landing and knocked on the door of McMahon, the schoolteacher. He closed the door behind them. While he felt around under her clothes, she watched herself in the mirrored door of his wardrobe. She could see that they were right. She was different. The dreamy look had gone from her eyes. Her legs were getting a shape of their own. Even her chest, which the schoolteacher smoothed with chalky fingers, had developed a springy feel. With her hair up her face looked stange. They'd never leave her alone now. She was pretty.

She felt no better afterwards, although no worse, and went outside for a cry in the lavatory. When she emerged into the yard a big lumpy cat was sitting on the wall, looking down at her. 'You're in trouble,' she noticed, 'ain't you?' She held out her arms and the animal made a leap that looked suicidal but the child managed to catch it. 'They won't let me keep you,' Frankie told the creature, but the rumbling warmth relieved her aching arms. She carried it upstairs. There was nowhere to hide it so she stood on the bed as Lena had done and hoisted the cat up into the Christmas crib.

That night when she was damping down the fires, a

terrible bawling came from her room. Frankie flew up the stairs, her boots barely grazing the steps. Lena must have found the cat. She must be having a fit.

She wasn't having a fit. Frankie grinned when she saw the fat girl stranded on the bed, her ringlets pinned to her wet red forehead and howls flying from her mouth like bats from a cave. She was having her baby.

'I'm poisoned. I'm dyin',' Lena gasped.

'You're all right,' Frankie dabbed at Lena's forehead with the end of her pinafore. 'Your baby's coming.'

Lena stopped bawling to gape at her. 'What are you on about?'

'You can't keep it hid no more,' Frankie said. 'I knew from the first minute I saw you, you was having a baby.'

'You know nothing! You're just pig ignorant,' Lena whimpered. 'How could I be having a baby an' I not even married?'

'Don't you have no brothers and sisters?' Frankie began to tear up her sheet. 'Ain't you never seen your mam havin' a baby?'

'I be's from the orphanage,' Lena said. 'I can't be havin' a baby. I bein't married.'

Frankie sighed. 'Take long breaths and try not to make a racket. I'll tell ma'am you've got a colic.'

Mrs Deveney sat up in bed plucking the beads of her rosary as if tearing leeches from her flesh. 'Lena is poorly, ma'am, but she don't need a doctor,' Frankie said.

'No,' Mrs Deveney said; 'no doctor. She is as strong as a

horse.'

After four hours a baby boy came. Puce and mummified the infant gave a thrilling cry and Frankie washed him in the bucket of warm water she had dragged up from the kitchen and laid him on her pillow. When she had him settled she turned to comfort Lena and saw that the girl was in labour again. Close to morning a little girl came and the needling cry was answered by a bird from the dawn roofs.

For a long time Frankie could only stare at them. No humans could be so perfect, so perfectly matched. They even had hair, black and silky thistledown tufts. Although she hadn't slept all night, their creamy sleep restored her. She lay down for a little while beside them on the bed and then she went downstairs to light the range.

She had to make the breakfasts herself that morning and clear up after them so it was ten o'clock before she could get back upstairs with tea for Lena.

Lena was gone. The bloody rags and bucket were gone. The babies were missing.

At lunchtime, when the cook returned, she climbed into bed in all her clothes and sullenly stared at the wall.

'Where are the babies?' Frankie said.

'What babies?' Lena heaved around to face her. 'I was poisoned by a bad sassidge. I been to the doctor and he said to stay in bed.'

'Twins,' Frankie said. 'I washed them myself and put them on my bed.'

'Well there be's no twins now and no bucket neither and   39 you better stop behaving like a demented herrin'.'

'I didn't mention the bucket,' Frankie said.

Lena sat up in bed and screeched at her. 'There was no bucket!'

And suddenly Frankie knew. She knew. She saw the little hands grasping at the bloody water, so familiar from their recent swimming home, the dark fronds of their hair rising to the oily surface to explore the air.

'I know there were babies,' she glanced around the room as if looking for a clue and her eyes came to rest on the cat in the crib, who had maintained her conspiracy of silence throughout the howling night. The cat kneaded the straw and blinked at her. 'Twins.'

'You know nothin', Hokey,' Lena said; 'and there bein't nothin' you can do about it neither.'

Downstairs Mrs Deveney was already up and scrubbing a bucket in the yard. She was giving out about Lena's idleness. She thought she might dispatch her back to the nuns. When she saw the way Frankie was looking at her, the yellow of her skin became tinged with ash. 'Go into the kitchen now and get yourself a little egg,' she said and dragged her lips down towards reluctant mirth.

A week after Lena went back to scrub for the nuns Frankie's cat gave birth to three kittens in the straw. She had never seen new-born kittens before. Their tiny paws, like blackberries, and blunt, bad-tempered snouts enchanted her. Her mother told her that people drown kittens in a bucket, but she didn't believe it. No one would do such a thing.

'Any road,' she told herself, 'I'll keep them hid.' Her employer seemed older since Lena's departure. Maybe she wouldn't bother with the long climb all the way up to the attic.

It was the little girl's first Christmas away from home. She couldn't leave. It wasn't just the kittens. With no other help in the house Mrs Deveney needed her.

She got two shillings from McMahon the schoolteacher and spent it on a basket of oranges with silver paper around the handle, and halfpennies hidden in the fruit. She sent this by messenger to her house, with a bottle of port for her ma and da.

In the morning she cooked the Christmas dinner for Mrs Deveney and McMahon, swathed in a big holland apron which showed off her waist. Afterwards she stole milk for the mother cat and a glass of sherry for herself and went upstairs to play with the kittens.

They kneaded their mother with the tiny thorns of their claws, tumbling on the bed where she had imagined twins to have proceeded from the beguiling fatness of Lena the cook. She was all right now. Mrs Deveney got her violet powder for her nightmares.

She picked up the kittens and held them to her chest. They depended on her. She loved them more than all the world. She still knew nothing, but she was learning. Refinement and religion, you picked them up as you went along.

The three kittens were different colours – yellow, and striped and a black one swirled with white stars like the star that had led the wise men to Bethlehem with their gifts of inestimable value. She named them Gold and Frankincense and Myrrh.

The Stolen Child

Women steal other people's husbands so why shouldn't they steal other people's babies? Mothers leave babies everywhere. They leave them with foreign students while they go out gallivanting, hand them over to strangers for years on end, who stuff them with dead languages and computer science. I knew a woman who left her baby on the bus. She was halfway down Grafton Street when she got this funny feeling and she said, 'Oh, my God, I've left my handbag,' and then with a surge of relief she felt the strap of her bag cutting into her wrist and remembered the baby.

I never wanted to steal another woman's husband. Whatever you might make of a man if you got him first-hand, there's no doing anything once some other woman's been at him, started scraping off the first layer of paint to see what's underneath, then decided she didn't like it, and left him like that all scratchy and patchy.

Babies come unpainted. They have their own smell, like new wood has. They've got no barriers. Mothers go at their offspring the way a man goes at a virgin, no shame or mercy. A woman once told me she used to bite her baby's bum when she changed its nappy. Other women have to stand back, but nature's nature.

Sometimes I dream of babies. Once there were two in a wooden cradle high up on a shelf. They had very small dark faces, like Russian icons, and I climbed on a chair to get at them. Then I saw their parents sitting up in bed, watching me. I have a dream about a little girl, three or four, who runs behind to catch up with me. She says nothing but her hand burrows into mine and her fingers tap on my palm. Now and then I have a baby in my sleep, although I don't remember anything about it. It's handed to me, and I know it's mine, and I just gaze into the opaque blueness of the eye that's like the sky, as if everything and nothing lies behind.

It comes over you like a craving. You stand beside a pram and stare the way a woman on a diet might stare at a bar of chocolate in a shop window. You can't say anything. It's taboo, like cannibalism. Your middle goes hollow and you walk away stiff-legged, as if you have to pee.

Or maybe you don't.

It happened just like that. I'd come out of the supermarket. There were three infants, left lying around in strollers. I stopped to put on my headscarf and I looked at the babies, the way people do. I don't know what did it to me, but I think it was the texture. There was this chrysalis look. I was wondering what they felt like. To tell the truth my mouth was watering just for a touch. Then one of them turned with jerky movements to look at me.

'Hello,' I said. She stirred in her blankets and blew a tiny bubble. She put out a toe to explore the air. She looked so new, so completely new, that I was mad to have her. It's like when you see some dress in a shop window and you have to have it because you think it will definitely change your life. Her skin was rose soft and I had a terrible urge to touch it. 'Plenty of time for that,' I thought as my foot kicked the brake of the pram.

Mothers don't count their blessings. They complain all the time and they resent women without children, as if they've got away with something. They see you as an alien species. Talk about a woman scorned! And it's not men who scorn you. They simply don't notice you at all. It's other women who treat you like the cat daring to look at the king. They don't care for women like me, they don't trust us. Well, I don't like them much either.

I was at the bus stop one day and this woman came along with a toddler by the hand and a baby in a push-car. 'Terrible day!' I said. Well it was. Cats and dogs. She gave me a look as if she was about to ask for a search warrant and then turned away and commenced a performance of pulling up hoods and shoving on mittens. It wasn't the rain. She didn't even notice the rain, soaked to the bone, hair stuck to her head like a bag of worms. She had all this shopping, spilling out of plastic bags, and she bent down and began undoing her parcels, arranging them in the tray underneath the baby's seat, as if to say to me, 'This is our world. We don't need your sort.' Not that I need telling.

It was a relief when the bus came – but that was short-lived. I don't know why mothers can't be more organized. She hoisted the toddler on to the platform and then got up herself, leaving the baby all alone in the rain to register its despair. 'You've forgotten the baby,' I said, and she gave me a very dirty look. She lunged outward and seized the handles of the pram and tried to manhandle it up after her, but was too heavy. Sullen as mud, she plunged back out into the rain. This time the toddler was abandoned on the bus and it opened its little mouth and set up a pitiful screeching. She unstrapped the baby and sort of flung it up on the bus. Everyone was looking. Back she clambered, leaned out again and wrestled the pram on board, as if some sort of battle to the death was involved. I don't think the woman was in her right mind. Of course, half the groceries fell out into the gutter and the baby followed. 'You're going about that all wrong,' I told her, but she took no notice. The driver then woke up and said he couldn't take her as there was already one push-car on the bus. Do you think she apologized for keeping everyone waiting? No! She merely gave me a most unpleasant glance, as if I was the one to blame.

Walking away from the supermarket with someone else's child, I didn't feel guilty. I was cleansed, absolved of the guilt of not fitting in. I loved that baby. I felt connected to her by all the parts that unglamorous single women aren't supposed to have. I believed we were allies. She seemed to understand that I needed her more than her mother did and I experienced a great well of pity for her helplessness. She could do nothing without me and I would do anything in the world for her. I wheeled the pram out through the car park, not too quickly. Once I even stopped to settle her blankets. Oh, she was the sweetest thing. Several people smiled into the pram. When I gave her a little tickle, she laughed. I think I have a natural talent as a mother. I look at other women with their kids and think, 'She's doing that all wrong, she doesn't deserve to have her.' I notice things. The worst mothers are the ones with too many kids. Just like my mum. They bash them and yell at them and then they give them sweets. Just like this woman I saw watching me from the doorway of the supermarket. She seemed completely surrounded by children. There must have been seven of them. One kid was being belted by another and a third was scuttling off out under a car. And she just watched me intently with this pinched little face and I knew she was envying me my natural ease as a mother. I knew a widow once, used to leave her baby in the dog's basket with the dog when she went out to work.

And all this time, while I was pushing and plotting, where was her mother? She might have been in the newsagent's, flipping the pages of magazines, or giving herself a moustache of cappuccino in the coffee shop, or in the supermarket gazing at bloated purple figs and dreaming of a lover. Mothers, who swear that they would die in an instant for you, are never there when you need them. Luckily, there is frequently someone on hand, as for instance myself, who was now wheeling the poor little thing out of harm's way, 47 and not, if you ask me, before time.

I can't remember ever being so happy. There was a sense of purpose, the feeling of being needed. And you'll laugh now, but for the first time in my life, looking into that sweet little face, I felt that I was understood.

When my mum died I got depressed and they sent me along to see a psychiatrist. He said to me, 'You're young. You have to make a life of your own.' I was furious. 'Hardly anyone makes a life of their own,' I told him. 'They get their lives made for them.' He asked me about my social life and I said I went to the pictures once in a while. 'You could put an advertisement in one of the personal columns,' he said.

'Advertisement for what?' I said.

'A companion,' he said.

'Just like that?' I must say I thought that was a good one. 'You put an advertisement in the paper and you get a companion?' I pictured a fattish little girl of about ten with long plaits.

'People do,' he promised me. 'Or you could go to an introduction agency.'

'And what sort of thing would you say in this advertisement?'

'You could say you were an attractive woman, early thirties, seeking kind gentleman friend, view to matrimony.'

I was so mad. I lashed out at him with my handbag. 'You said a companion. You never said anything about a gentleman friend.'

Well, I make out all right. I got a bit of part-time work and I took up a hobby. I became a shoplifter. Many people are compelled to do things that are outside their moral strictures in these straitened times, but personally I took to shoplifting like a duck to water. It gave me a lift and enabled me to sample a lot of interesting things. The trick is, you pay for the bulky items and put away the small ones, fork out for the sliced loaf, pinch the kiwi fruit, proffer for the potatoes, take the pâté, pay for the firelighters, stash the little tray of fillet steaks. In this way I added a lot of variety to my diet – lumpfish roe and anchovies and spiced olives and smoked salmon, although I also accumulated a lot of sliced bread. 'Use your imagination,' I told myself. 'There are other bulky items besides sliced loaves.'

Perhaps it was the pack of nappies in my trolley that did it. I hate waste. It also just happened that the first sympathetic face I saw that day (in years, in point of fact) was that tiny baby left outside in her pram to wave her toe around in the cold air, so I took her too.

I thought I'd call her Vera. It sounded like the name of a person who'd been around for a long time, or as if I'd called her after my mother. When I got home the first thing I did was to pick her up. Oh, she felt just lovely, like nothing at all. I went over to the mirror to see what kind of a pair we made. We looked a picture. She took years off my age.

Vera was looking around in a vaguely disgruntled way, as if she could smell burning. 'Milk,' I thought. 'She wants milk.' I kept her balanced on my arm while I warmed up some milk. It was a nice feeling, although inconvenient. I would have to get used to that. It was like smoking in the bath. I had to carry her back with the saucepan, and a spoon, and a dishtowel for a bib. Natural mothers don't have to ferret around with saucepans and spoons. They have everything to hand, inside their slip. I tried to feed her off a spoon but she blew at it instead of sucking. There was milk in my hair and on my cardigan and quite a lot of it went on the sofa, which is a kingfisher pattern, blue on cream. After a while she pushed the cup away and her face folded up as if she was going to cry. 'Oh, sorry, sweetheart,' I said. 'Who's a stupid mummy?' She needed her nappy changed.

To tell the truth I had been looking forward to this. Women complain about the plain duties of motherhood but to me she was like a present that was waiting to be unwrapped. I carried her back downstairs and filled a basin with warm water and put a lot of towels over my arm. How did I manage this, you ask? Well, a trail of water from kitchen to sofa tells the tale – but I managed the talc and the nappies and a sponge and all the other bits and pieces. I was proud of myself. I almost wished there was someone there to see.

By now Vera was a bit uneasy (perhaps I should have played some music, like women do to babies in the womb, but I don't know much about music). I took off the little pink jacket, the pink romper suit that was like a hot-water-bottle cover and then started to unwrap the nappy. A jet of water shot up into my eye. I was startled and none too pleased. I rubbed my eye and and began again, removing all that soggy padding. Then I slammed it shut. The child looked gratified and started to chortle. Incredulous, I peeled the swaddling back once more. My jaw hung off its hinges. Growing out of the bottom of its belly was a wicked little ruddy horn. I found myself looking at balls as big as pomegranates and when I could tear my eyes away from them I had to look into his eye, a man's eye, already calculating and bargaining.

It was a boy. Who the hell wants a boy?

'Hypocrite!' I said to him. 'Going round with that nice little face.'

Vera stuck out his lower lip.

Imagine the nerve of the mother, dressing him up in pink, palming him off as a girl! Imagine, I could still be taken in by a man.

Now the problem with helping yourself to things, as opposed to coming by them lawfully, is that you have no redress. You have to take what you get. On the other hand, as a general rule, this makes you less particular. I decided to play it cool. 'The thing is, Vera,' I told him (I would change his name later. The shock was too great to adjust to all at once), 'I always thought of babies as female. It simply never occurred to me that they came in the potential rapist mode. Now, clearly there are points in your favour. You do look very nice with all your clothes on. On the other hand, I can't take to your sort as a species.'

I was quite pleased with that. I thought it very moderate   51 and rational. Vera was looking at me in the strangest way, with a sweet, intent, intelligent look. Clearly he was concentrating. There is something to be said for the intelligent male. Maybe he and I would get along. 'The keynote,' I told him, 'is compromise. We'll have to give each other plenty of space.' Vera smiled. He looked relieved. It was a weight off my mind too. Then I got this smell. It dawned on me with horror the reason for his concentration. 'No!' I moaned. 'My mother's Sanderson!' I swooped on him and swagged him without looking too closely. His blue eyes no longer seemed opaque and new but very old and angry. He opened his mouth and began to bawl. Have you ever known a man who could compromise?

All that afternoon I gazed in wonder on the child who had melted my innards and compelled me to crime. Within the space of half an hour he had been transformed. His face took on the scalded red of a baboon's behind and he bellowed like a bull. His eyes were brilliant chips of ice behind a wall of boiling water. I got the feeling it wasn't even personal. It was just what he did whenever he thought of it. I changed his nappy and bounced him on my knee until his brains must have scrambled. I tried making him a mush of bread and milk and sugar, which he scarcely touched, yet still managed to return in great quantity over my ear. With rattling hands I strapped him into the stroller and took him for a walk. Out of doors the noise became a metallic booming. People glared at me and moved away and crows fell off their perches in the trees. Everything seemed distorted by the sound. I felt quite mad with tiredness. My legs seemed to be melting and when I looked at the sky the clouds had a fizzing, dangerous look. I wanted to lie flat on the pavement. You can't when you're a mother. Your life's not your own any more. I realized now that the mother-and-child unit is not the one I imagined but a different kind in which she exists to keep him alive and he exists to keep her awake.

I hadn't had a cup of tea all day, or a pee. When I got home there was a note on the door. It was from my landlord, asking had I a child concealed on the premises. Concealment, I mirthlessly snorted, would be a fine thing. He said it was upsetting the other tenants and either it went or I did.

I crept in to turn on the news. By now Vera would be reported missing. His distraught mother would come on the telly begging whoever had him to please let her have her baby back. It was difficult to hear above the infant shrieks but I could see Bill Clinton's flashing teeth and bodies in the streets in Bosnia and men in suits at EEC summits. I watched until the weatherman had been and gone. Vera and I wept in unison. Was this what they meant by bonding?

Some time in the night the crying stopped. The crimson faded from my fledgling's cheek and he subsided into rosy sleep. There was a cessation in the hostile shouts and banging on walls from neighbours. I sat over him and stroked his little fluff of hair and his cheek that was like the inside of a flower and then I must have fallen asleep for I dreamed I was being ripped apart by slash hooks but I woke up and it was his barking cries slicing through the fibres of my nerves.

Vera beamed like a rose as I wheeled him back to the supermarket. Daylight lapped around me like a great, dangerous, glittering sea. After twenty-four hours of torture I had entered a twilight zone and was both light-headed and depressed so that tears slid down my face as I exulted at the endurance of the tiny creature in my custody, the dazzling scope of his language of demand which ranged from heart-rending mews to the kind of frenzied sawing sounds which might have emanated from the corpse stores of Dr Frankenstein, from strangled croaks to the foundation-rattling bellows of a Gargantua. He had broken me. My nerve was gone and even my bones felt loose. I had to concentrate, in the way a drunk does, on setting my feet one in front of the other. I parked him carefully outside the supermarket and even did some shopping, snivelling a bit as I tucked away a little tin of white crab meat for comfort. Then I was free. I urged my trembling limbs to haste. 'You've forgotten your baby!' a woman cried out. My boneless feet tried an ineffectual scarper and the wheels of the push-car squealed in their pursuant haste. Upset by the crisis, the baby began to yell.

There are women who abandon babies in phone booths and lavatories and on the steps of churches, but these are

stealthy babies, silently complicit in their own desertion.

Vera was like a burglar alarm in reverse. Wherever I set him down, he went off. I tried cafés, cinemas, police stations. Once, I placed him in a wastepaper basket and he seemed to like that, for there wasn't a peep, but then when I was scurrying off down the street, I remembered that vandals sometimes set fire to refuse bins, so I ran back and fished him out. At the end of the day we went home and watched the news in tears. There was no report of a baby missing. Vera's cries seemed to have been slung like paint around the walls so that even in his rare sleeping moments they remained violent and vivid and neighbours still hammered on the walls. Everyone blamed me. It was like being harnessed to a madman. It reminded me of something I had read, how in Victorian almshouses, sane paupers were frequently chained to the bed with dangerous lunatics.

By the third day I could think of nothing but rest. Sleep became a lust, an addiction. I was weeping and twitching and creeping on hands and knees. I wanted to lie down somewhere dark and peaceful where the glaring cave of my baby's mouth could no more pierce me with its proclamations. Then, with relief, I remembered the river-bed. No one would find me there. Feverishly I dressed the child and wheeled him to the bridge. We made our farewells and I was about to hop into oblivion when I noticed a glove, left on one of the spikes that ornament the metalwork, so that whoever had lost it would spot it right away. It was an inspiration, a sign from God. I lifted Vera on to the broad ledge of the bridge, hooked his little jumper on to a spike, 55 and left him there, peering quite serenely into the water.

At the end of the bridge I turned and looked back. The baby had disappeared. Someone had taken him. It seemed eerily quiet without that little soul to puncture the ozone with his lungs. Then I realized just why it was so quiet. There wasn't a someone. There hadn't been anyone since I left him there.

I raced back. 'Vera!' There was no sound, and when I gazed into the water it offered back an ugly portrait of the sky.

'Vera!' I wailed.

After a few seconds the baby surfaced. At first he bounced into view and bobbed in the water, waiting to get waterlogged and go down again. Then he reached out an arm as if there was an object in the murky tide he wanted. He didn't seem frightened. There was something leisurely about that outstretched hand, the fingers slightly curled, like a woman reaching for a cake. He began to show signs of excitement. His little legs started to kick. Out went another arm towards an unseen goal. 'What are you doing?' I peered down into the filthy water in which no other living thing was. Up came the arm again, grabbed the water and withdrew. His feet kicked in delight. The baby's whole body looked delighted. I moved along the wall, following his progress, trying to see what he saw, that made him rejoice. Then I realized; he was swimming. The day was still and there was very little current. He gained confidence with every stroke. 'Wait!' I kept pace along the wall. The baby took no notice. He had commenced his new life as a fish. 'Wait!' I cried. For me, I meant. I wanted to tell him he was wonderful, that I would forgive him all his smells and yowling for in that well-defended casement was a creature capable of new beginnings. He did not strike out at the water as adults do but used his curled hands as scoops, and his rounded body as a floating ball. He was merely walking on the water like Jesus, or crawling since he had not yet learned to walk. 'Wait!' I begged as he bobbed past once again. I threw off my raincoat and jumped into the water. As I stretched out to reach the little curving fingers, he began to snarl.

I would like to report a happy ending, but then too I have always hankered for a sighting of a hog upon the wing. It took five more days to locate the mother. She told the police she had had a lovely little holiday by the sea and thought their Clint was being safely looked after by a friend, who, like everyone else in her life, had let her down. As it transpired, I knew the mother and she knew me, although we did not refresh our acquaintance. It was the pinched little women with all the kids who had watched me wheel her child away. She said their Clint was a bawler, she hadn't had a wink of sleep since the day he was born, but she would take him back if someone gave her a Walkman to shut out the noise. Nobody bothered about me, the heroine of the hour – a woman who had risked her life to save a drowning child. It was the mother who drew the limelight. She became a sort of cult figure for a while and mothers could be spotted everywhere smiling under earphones, just as they used to waddle about in tracksuits a year or two ago. It was left to us, the childless, to suffer the curdling howls of the nation's unattended innocents.

Some women don't deserve to have children.

A Note on Clare Boylan

Clare Boylan was born and grew up in Dublin, which is the setting for two of her novels. An award-winning journalist, she turned to fiction, enjoying widespread success with her short stories, which have been adapted into films and published in many countries as well as in her collection *A Nail on the Head*. After a career that has included playwriting, radio and television broadcasting, close-harmony singing, editing two magazines, book-selling and cutting the heads off cabbages in the back room of a grocery shop, she now confines herself to short and long fiction, cats, literary criticism and some journalism. Her three novels, *Holy Pictures*, *Last Resorts* and *Black Baby*, are published by Penguin.

Clare Boylan lives in Wicklow with her journalist husband.